For Kevin,
who would rather tickle a dragon than fight one.
—D. B.

To Betsy and Jeff Woytovich
and my CAP (Children's Alopecia Project) friends.
Again proving that "not typical" can be the most special.
—T. B.

VIKING
Published by the Penguin Group
Penguin Young Readers Group, 345 Hudson Street, New York, New York 10014, U.S.A.
Penguin Group (Canada), 90 Eglinton Avenue East, Suite 700, Toronto, Ontario, Canada M4P 2Y3
(a division of Pearson Penguin Canada Inc.)
Penguin Books Ltd, 80 Strand, London WC2R 0RL, England
Penguin Ireland, 25 St Stephen's Green, Dublin 2, Ireland (a division of Penguin Books Ltd)
Penguin Group (Australia), 250 Camberwell Road, Camberwell, Victoria 3124, Australia
(a division of Pearson Australia Group Pty Ltd)
Penguin Books India Pvt Ltd, 11 Community Centre, Panchsheel Park, New Delhi – 110 017, India
Penguin Group (NZ), 67 Apollo Drive, Rosedale, Auckland 0632, New Zealand (a division of Pearson New Zealand Ltd.)
Penguin Books (South Africa) (Pty) Ltd, 24 Sturdee Avenue, Rosebank, Johannesburg 2196, South Africa

Penguin Books Ltd, Registered Offices: 80 Strand, London WC2R 0RL, England

First published in the United States of America by Viking, a division of Penguin Young Readers Group, 2013

10   9   8   7   6   5   4   3   2

Text copyright © Dan Bar-el, 2013
Illustrations copyright © Tim Bowers, 2013
All rights reserved

LIBRARY OF CONGRESS CATALOGING-IN-PUBLICATION DATA
Bar-el, Dan.
Not your typical dragon / by Dan Bar-el ; illustrated by Tim Bowers.
p. cm.
Summary: "When Crispin Blaze turns seven, he's expected to breathe fire like all the other dragons. But instead
of fire, he breathes a host of unusual things"—Provided by publisher.
ISBN 978-0-670-01402-6 (hardcover)
[1. Dragons—Fiction. 2. Individuality—Fiction. 3. Self-acceptance—Fiction.] I. Bowers, Tim, ill. II. Title.
PZ7.B250315No 2013
[E]—dc23
2012014391

Manufactured in China
Set in Hadriano Std   Book design by Jim Hoover
The illustrations for this book are rendered in acrylic paint on illustration board.

And then he jumped up and danced to Crispin's music, too.

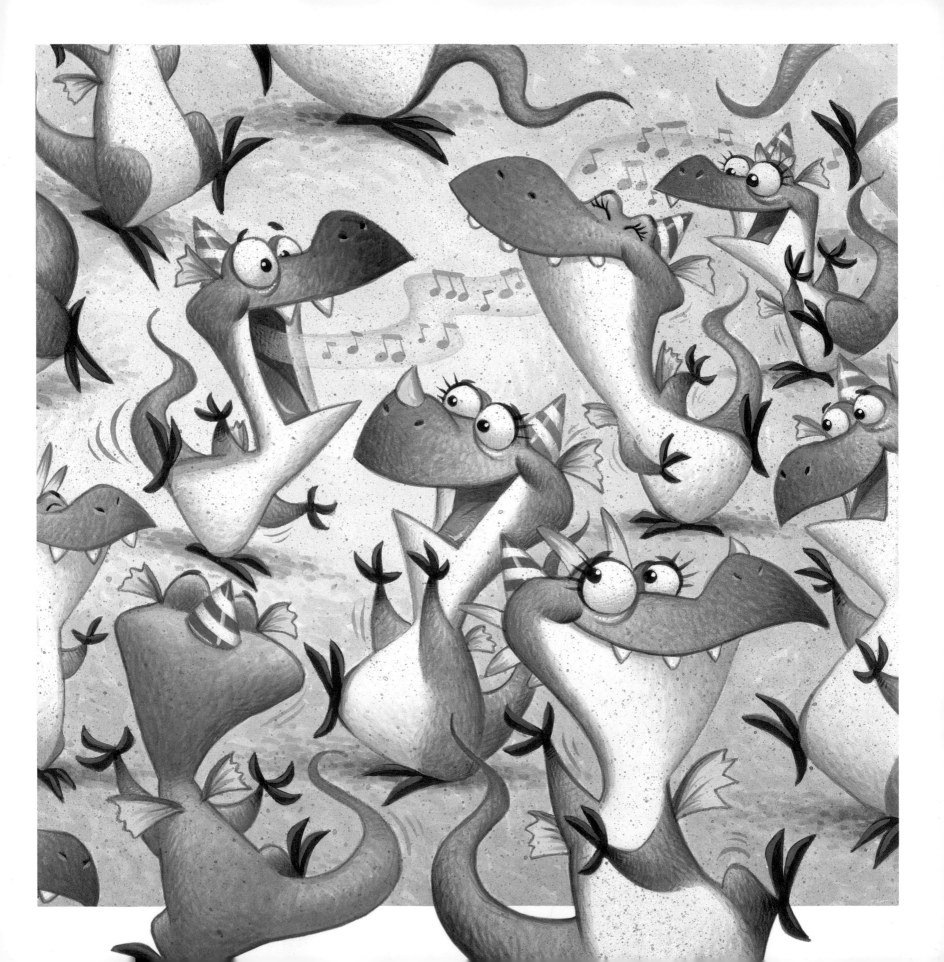

On Crispin's next birthday, there was a big party. Family and friends came from all over the land. Sir George and his family came, too.

Lots of dragons were dancing. Crispin stood with his mouth open wide. Fire still did not come out. Music came out instead.

"Your son," said an old uncle to Crispin's father, "he's not your typical dragon, is he?"

"No," replied Crispin's father proudly. "My son is something special."

A gush of water shot out!

Crispin aimed the water at his father's flames. He saved his home, and he even saved the shiny man, who wasn't looking so shiny anymore.

"Hurray for Crispin!" everyone shouted.

"Do your worst, dragon!" declared the shiny man.

But then the flames scorched the lawn.

"That's enough, honey," said Crispin's mother.

The flames singed the fence.

"You've made your point, dear, now stop showing off," she scolded.

Then the flames ignited the roof.

Crispin's father panicked. "I can't stop breathing fire!"

"You'll burn our house down!" cried his mother. "You'll burn down the whole neighborhood!"

Dragons came running from all directions. They knew how to start fires, but no one knew how to stop them.

Crispin suddenly felt a tingling in his tummy. He felt a bubbling in his belly. He opened his mouth.

But fire did not come out.

"A dragon that doesn't breathe fire? That's the silliest thing I've ever heard." The shiny man laughed.

Crispin's father stormed out of the house. "My son is not silly! He may not breathe fire, but I certainly do!"

Crispin's father let out a powerful spray of flames.

Crispin's parents were relieved when he arrived home safely. Sir George was about to say good-bye when they heard a shout.

"There you are, boy! Why on earth are you playing with a fire-breathing dragon?"

"He's my friend, Father," whispered Sir George, "and besides, he doesn't breathe fire."

Secretly, Sir George was glad that Crispin couldn't breathe fire. He liked the little dragon and didn't want to fight him. Crispin liked the shiny knight, too, but he missed his parents. "Sir George, it's getting dark. I want to go home."

The shiny knight patted him on the back. "Don't worry, little dragon. I will take you."

But Sir George was not ready to give up. "Aha! The book says you're too stressed."

Sir George made Crispin close his eyes while he described a quiet, relaxing day at the ocean. "Do you feel calm? Now imagine a hundred shiny knights attacking you!"

Crispin opened his mouth. But fire did not come out. Beach balls came out.

"Well, that's just plain weird."

Sir George searched through the book again. "Aha! It says it's probably your attitude."

Sir George showed Crispin how to look mean and angry enough to breathe fire.

Crispin opened his mouth. But fire did not come out.

Soft, cuddly teddy bears came out.

"Hmmm," said Sir George, "we may have taken a step backward."

"It's no use," Crispin sighed. "I'm just not your typical dragon."

Red party streamers came out.

"At least they're the right color," said Sir George kindly.

"Of course!" Sir George searched through the pages. "It says it's probably just your diet."

Sir George fed Crispin spicy curry, scorching chili, and blistering salsa.

Crispin opened his mouth. But fire did not come out.

Soap bubbles came out.

"Don't you breathe fire, dragon?"

Crispin shook his head. "I can't."

Sir George moaned. "But my father insists that I fight a fire-breathing dragon. It even says here in my book that your typical dragon breathes fire."

"I'm not your typical dragon," Crispin explained.

Sir George sighed. "I can't go home."

"Me neither." Crispin nodded. But then he had an idea. "Maybe your book could tell us what to do."

"I am Sir George," squeaked a thin, shiny knight. "Sh-sh-show yourself, dragon!"

Crispin shuffled out of the cave.

The thin, shiny knight held up his thin, shiny sword. "D-d-do your worst, dragon!"

Crispin opened his mouth. But fire did not come out.

The world can be a scary place for a little dragon who can't breathe fire.

Crispin found a dark cave. "I'll be a fireless dragon all by myself. I won't bother anyone, and no one will bother me."

An hour later, he had a visitor.

Marshmallows came out.

"Dragons breathe fire!" yelled the coach. "Isn't that right, class?"

The other dragons didn't answer. They were too busy looking for pointy sticks for marshmallow roasting.

I guess I'm not a real dragon, Crispin thought. He worried that his family would be disappointed.

So he ran away from home.

Band-Aids came out.

"I see," said the doctor gravely.

"Dragons should breathe fire," insisted Crispin's father.

"We were low on Band-Aids," mumbled the nurse.

The doctor sent Crispin home with medicine. He swallowed two teaspoons before going to school.

"It will help you become a real dragon," said his father with a wink.

After school, Crispin joined his first fire breathing practice. One by one, little dragons aimed their fiery breath at stacks of logs until they burst into flames.

Crispin stepped up confidently. He could feel the medicine bubbling in his belly. But when he opened his mouth, fire did not come out.

Whipped cream came out.

"Crispin!" shouted his father. "Dragons breathe fire!"

"What will the neighbors think?" worried his mother.

"I love whipped cream," said his little sister Ashley.

The little dragon was whisked off to the doctor the very next day.

"Please fix my son," demanded Crispin's father.

"What seems to be the problem?" asked the doctor.

Crispin opened his mouth and breathed. But fire did not come out.

The next day, Crispin sat among family and friends as a big cake was brought to the table.

"Who will light the birthday candles?" his mother asked.

"I will!" declared Crispin. He could feel a tingling inside his tummy. But when he opened his mouth, fire did not come out.

The little dragon imagined all the forests he would burn down. He dreamed of all the castles he would destroy. He also considered boiling water to make tea, but he didn't tell his father that.

Crispin Blaze was born into a proud family of fire-breathing dragons.

"Every Blaze breathes fire," explained his father. "I breathe fire. Your mother breathes fire. Tomorrow, when you turn seven, you'll breathe fire, too."

Not Your Typical Dragon

by
Dan Bar-el

illustrated by
Tim Bowers

VIKING
An Imprint of Penguin Group (USA) Inc.